A Waste of Space

BILL CONDON

Illustrated by Coral Tulloch

D1490781

 sundance

Published by
Sundance Publishing
234 Taylor Street
Littleton, MA 01460

Copyright © text Bill Condon
Copyright © illustrations Coral Tulloch
Project commissioned and managed by
Lorraine Bambrough-Kelly, The Writer's Style
Designed by Cath Lindsey/design rescue

First published 1998 by
Addison Wesley Longman Australia Pty Limited
95 Coventry Street
South Melbourne 3205 Australia
Exclusive United States Distribution: Sundance Publishing

ISBN 0-7608-3294-3

Printed in China

Contents

To my cousin, Winnie Laycock, with love.

CHAPTER 1

The Giant

Louella towered over her classmates like a giraffe at a pygmy picnic.

"What's the weather like up there?" asked Sally Anne.

"Watch out for low-flying planes," joked Anthony.

As well as being tall, Louella was paper-thin. Her classmates told her that she should stay inside on windy days so she wouldn't get blown away.

She was clumsy and gangly, too. When she
ran, her legs twirled like propellers, and she
flung her arms around as if she were
swatting at a swarm of bees.

It was much worse on Thursdays. All because of softball.

Each week the gym teacher, Mr. Robinson, picked two captains, who were then told to choose teams.

Louella would stand like a puppy in a pet shop window, hoping to be chosen. But when the teams were picked, she was always the one no one wanted.

CHAPTER 2

The Little Brother

"What's wrong with me?" Louella asked her mother.

"Not a single thing."

"But I want everyone to like me, Mom, and no one does."

Her little brother, Luke, stopped watching television just long enough to say, "I know why no one likes you, Louella."

"Why?"

"Because you're a waste of space!"

Luke always said things like that. His mouth was always getting him into trouble, but that didn't stop him. It was his way of getting back at Louella for beating him in arm wrestling and running.

"It's just something he heard on TV," Mom said. "Pay no attention."

But the more Louella tried to ignore him, the harder Luke tried to annoy her.

"Waste of space, waste of space," he chanted, until Mom shooed him outside.

When he was gone, Louella said, "How can anyone as skinny as me be a waste of space? I hardly take up any room at all."

"How you look doesn't matter, Louella," Mom said. "It's how you feel inside that counts."

"But do you think I'm a waste of space?" Louella persisted.

Mom brushed her hand against Louella's cheek. "You know I don't. There are some people who are selfish and uncaring—they might be a waste of space, but you're not like that."

CHAPTER 3

Louella's a Vampire!

Later that afternoon, as Louella was all set to bite into the last piece of chocolate cake, she remembered her mother's words.

"I better not be selfish," she thought. "I'll give this piece of cake to Luke."

But instead of thanking her, Luke asked, "What's wrong with it?"

"Nothing, Luke."

He sniffed the cake suspiciously. "Did you put a cockroach in it?"

"There's nothing wrong with it, Luke. Believe me."

"Did you dip it in some mud?"

"No."

"Drop it in the toilet?"

"No!"

"I know—you let Topsy lick it!"

"I did not!"

"You did so!"

Louella finally lost it.

"Just eat it!" she screamed, shoving the cake into Luke's mouth.

"Help! Help! She's choking me! Aaaarrgghh!"

Mom hurried into the room to find Louella
and Luke on Luke's bed, clobbering each
other with pillows.

"Who started this?" Mom asked, seizing the pillows.

"I was only trying to be caring," Louella spluttered.

"Yeah, right! First she choked me with chocolate cake that was full of cockroaches, then she tried to bite my neck—Louella's a vampire!"

"He's your little brother," Mom said to Louella. "You're supposed to take care of him. Now say you're sorry."

"But, Mom . . . "

"Say you're sorry."

"All right." She paused. "Sorry, Luke," she said, not really meaning it.

Luke grinned, then chanted, "Waste of space, waste of space."

"Go outside and play," Mom ordered, staring hard at Luke.

Louella glared at Luke and muttered, "Little brothers should be banned."

No Little brothers here

CHAPTER 4

The Matchstick Man

When Louella looked out the window the next morning, the sun was shining brightly. High up in the sky were tiny clusters of pinkish clouds. She squinted at them and began to see faces—smiling clown faces.

Louella smiled, too. "It's going to be a good day," she told herself.

She was still happy an hour later when she climbed on the schoolbus. Then she saw the softball bats and realized it was Thursday. Sports day.

"Oh, no," she muttered, "softball!"

At the morning assembly, the principal, Mrs. Rowland, introduced a new teacher.

"This is Mr. Trudgett," she said.

"Hello, everyone," he replied. "I look forward to meeting you all."

He was long and skinny, with straight, black, greasy hair, thick glasses, a mouth like a trout, and a pointy nose. He wore a suit straight from a museum, and his voice was slow, deep, and rumbly, as if he were talking underwater.

Jason Peters whispered, "He's an alien."

"Aliens aren't as creepy as him," said Claire.

"He looks like a greasy matchstick," chuckled Allan.

Marika jumped about excitedly. "Let's call him Matchstick Man!" she said.

More and more nicknames were thought of, and soon the kids were covering their mouths to stop themselves from giggling.

Louella was sure Mr. Trudgett heard them laughing.

"I feel sorry for him," she thought. "I know exactly how he must feel."

CHAPTER 5

Crash!

After the assembly broke up, Louella quickly forgot about Mr. Trudgett. She had something else on her mind. All through her morning classes, she worried about softball. She felt sick every time she thought about it.

"It's going to be another awful day," she told herself. "I know it."

Too soon, the dreaded hour arrived. Along with everyone else, she changed into her gym clothes and headed toward the ball field.

As they walked, Mr. Robinson, the gym teacher, challenged Jason and Anthony to a race.

"Ready, set, go!" Jason yelled, before Mr. Robinson and Anthony were ready.

"Here I come!" shouted Mr. Robinson, as he easily raced up to Jason and passed him.

He was well ahead when he turned around and shouted, "Can't you go any faster?"

"Watch out!" yelled Claire.

But Mr. Robinson didn't see the piece of wood.

Crash!

"Are you okay, sir?" asked Anthony.

Mr. Robinson struggled painfully to his feet. "I think so," he said, "but I better get my ankle checked out."

"Are we still going to play softball?" asked Mario.

Mr. Robinson nodded. "I'll send another teacher over. Meanwhile, you and Rachel can be the captains. Go ahead, choose your teams."

As Mr. Robinson hobbled away, a chorus of voices called to Rachel and Mario.

"Pick me."

"No, pick me."

"Hey, Mario, Rachel, over here, pick me . . . "

Louella looked down at her feet and wished she was somewhere else.

CHAPTER 6

The New Captains

Finally, she heard Mario say, "You take Louella, Rachel."

"No way! I don't want her on my team."

"Well, don't think I'm going to get stuck with her," Mario replied.

A screech from a whistle halted the argument. A lean, lanky figure approached.

"I'm in charge now," Mr. Trudgett said. "We won't be playing softball today. I don't like it very much."

Louella felt her heart somersault.

"Follow me," he said.

Rachel danced around in front of him. "Where are we going, sir?"

"To the basketball courts."

Mr. Trudgett's eyes focused on Louella. "The tall girl at the back," he said. "What's your name?"

"Louella, sir."

He smiled. "Okay, then. You're one of the captains. I'm the other one."

Mario stepped forward. "That's not fair."

"Yeah!" Rachel protested. "Mr. Robinson made Mario and me the captains."

Not even Count Dracula could have given them a creepier stare than Mr. Trudgett did.

Softly he said, "This is a new game, and it has new rules. My rules. Understand?"

"Yes, sir!" they said, almost as one.

Mr. Trudgett stuck his pointy nose in the air and strode off toward the basketball courts, with Louella right behind him.

CHAPTER 7

The Big Game

Not a word was spoken until they reached the courts. Then Mr. Trudgett produced an enormous toothy grin and told Louella, "Choose your team, Captain."

Louella felt fantastic. For the first time in her life, she was surrounded by girls and boys calling out:

"Pick me, Louella."

"No, pick me."

"Come on, Louella, pick me. Please!"

Louella looked past the kids at the front. Her first choices were those who, like her, were always the last to be picked.

After Mr. Trudgett picked his team, he asked the science teacher, Miss Puzo, to be the referee.

"Let's do it!" cried Miss Puzo, before blasting her whistle.

The game was on!

Louella nudged Claire. "What's a captain supposed to do?"

Claire shrugged. "How would I know? Just do it."

Louella was certain that everyone's eyes were trained on her, just waiting for her to make a dumb mistake.

But that was before Mr. Trudgett took off his sweatpants. Suddenly Louella's classmates were too busy looking at him to even think about her.

His skinny legs were so white they almost blinded everyone. And as he ran, his almost endless gorilla arms swung in every direction. But in a few moments, none of that mattered, because everyone realized he really knew how to play basketball.

Mr. Trudgett zigzagged all over the court, shooting three baskets in under a minute.

Just when it looked like he was going to score again, he stumbled, and the ball bounced over to Louella.

"Your turn," he said. "Let's see what you can do."

CHAPTER 8

The Cool Captain

Louella hesitated for a moment, then took off. Her long legs pumping, she ran along the outside of the court, bouncing the ball as she went.

"Gotcha!" cried Rachel, as she blocked Louella and grabbed for the ball.

"Shoot for the basket!" someone called.

Louella jumped up and hurled the ball toward the net. It hit the rim, spun around, and then like magic, dropped in.

"Yes! I did it!" she screamed.

And she didn't stop smiling for the rest of the game.

For the first time in Louella's life, being the tallest in the class was a huge advantage. When she leaped as high as she could, she could almost touch the basket rim.

"Pass the ball to Louella," yelled Claire.

Soon nearly everyone on her team was calling out the same thing. No wonder she scored a basket, then another, and (almost) another.

Finally, Miss Puzo blew the whistle to end the game.

"Sorry," she said, as she shook Louella's hand. "Your team loses by two points."

Louella didn't mind losing. Neither did her team. After all, they'd had a fantastic time.

"Well done, Louella," said Mr. Trudgett. "You were really good."

Louella gave a little smile, then looked away. But inside, she was jumping with joy. No one had *ever* said she was good at a sport before.

Then, when her teammates patted her on the back, she nearly fainted. "Yeah, good job, Louella," they said. "You're a cool captain."

Guess What?

Louella floated all the way home. It was the happiest day at school she could remember.

"Guess what, Mom?" she yelled, as soon as she raced in the door.

Words tumbled out of her mouth at the speed of lightning.

"We have a great new teacher, Mr. Trudgett, and we didn't play softball 'cause he said it was boring, and so, guess what? We played basketball! And I was the captain, Mom! Me! Captain! And guess what? I scored two baskets! And you know what else? You won't believe this—the other kids like me! They really like me!"

"They'd have to be very silly not to," said Mom.

Louella and her mom were both laughing when Luke shuffled into the room, his eyes wet with tears.

"What's wrong?" Mom asked.

"I got into a fight at school," he sniffled.

"What about?"

"Jeremy Scott picked on me. He said I've got a big nose. Do you think I have a big nose, Mom?"

"Of course you haven't, Luke. Has he, Louella?"

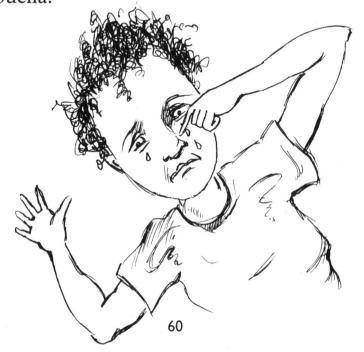

60

For one split second Louella was tempted to get even with Luke by telling him he had the biggest supersniffer on the planet. But then she recognized that sad look in his eyes—the look she usually had.

"Your nose is perfect," she told him.

"You mean it, Louella?"

"Sure," she smiled. "Anything less would be a waste of space."

Bill Condon

Bill Condon was one of fifteen children who grew up in a one-bedroom apartment. He had to grow up, because there wasn't room to grow sideways.

Like Louella, Bill is tall and thin, and like Luke, he has a big nose.

To cheer himself up, he once entered his nose in a beauty contest, but the judges didn't pick him — or his nose!

Coral Tulloch (that's me) lives on an island, with snow on the mountain in winter,.... And with her daughther Tully, her husband Peter and step-daughter Isabella,.... And with a ⟨rat⟩ Called Molly who likes to eat pasta,.... And a ⟨cat⟩ Called RED, who likes to eat boiled ⟨egg⟩'s & who you Can see on the ⟨island⟩ above ⟨egg⟩ & you Can SPY inside this ⟨book⟩. Tully likes to eat her ⟨egg⟩'s with faces drawn on them. Isabella likes chocolate ones. Coral likes spinach & Peter likes ⟨fish⟩ which is a good thing if you live on a street like ours with a pier at the end!